WORD BIRD
MAKES WORDS WITH CAT

by Jane Belk Moncure
illustrated by Linda Hohag

THE CHILD'S WORLD

ELGIN, ILLINOIS 60120

We acknowledge with gratitude the review of the Word Bird Short Vowel Adventure *books by Dr. John Mize, Director of Reading, Alamance County Schools, Graham, North Carolina.*

—The Child's World

Distributed by Childrens Press, 1224 West Van Buren Street, Chicago, Illinois 60607.

Library of Congress Cataloging in Publication Data

Moncure, Jane Belk.
  Word Bird makes words with Cat.
  — A short "a" adventure.

  (Word Bird's short vowel adventures)
  Summary: Word Bird makes a variety of words with his friend Cat. Each word that they make up leads them into a new activity.
  [1. Vocabulary.   2. Birds—Fiction.   3. Cats—Fiction]   I. Hohag, Linda, ill.   II. Title.
III. Series: Moncure, Jane Belk.   Word Bird's short vowel adventures.
PZ7.M739Wnc 1984   [E]   83-23948
ISBN 0-89565-259-5

1 2 3 4 5 6 7 8 9 10 11 12 R 91 90 89 88 87 86 85 84

WORD BIRD
MAKES WORDS WITH CAT

"What is in the box?" asked Word Bird one day.

"Word puzzles," said Papa.

"I can put word puzzles
together. I can make
words," said Word Bird.

Word Bird put

c with at

What word did he make?

c at

Just then Cat came to play.

"Hi, Cat."

"I can make words too," said Cat.

Cat put

r with at

What word did Cat make?

r at

Then Word Bird put

with

What word did he make?

"Let's play with hats,"
said Cat. And they did.

Then Word Bird put

with

What word did he make?

Cat put

p with an

What word did Cat make?

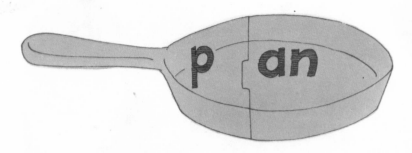

p an

Word Bird put

f with an

What word did he make?

f an

"I am hot," said Cat.
"Let's turn on the fan."

And they did.

Word Bird put

b with ag

What word did he make?

b ag

Cat put

fl with ag

What word did Cat make?

fl ag

"Let's make flags and let's march," said Word Bird.

They marched and
marched...

into the kitchen. Mama
gave them apples for
a snack.

"Let's make more words," said Word Bird. He put

c with ab

What word did he make?

c ab

"Let's go to the sandbox in my cab," said Word Bird.

"Let's play in the sand,"
said Cat. And they did.

They made sand roads...
lots of roads.

They made sand hills...
lots of hills.

They made a sand
castle too.

Word Bird was happy
because Cat did not
throw sand.

Cat sat and played
like a good cat.

Then Mama said, "Come here, Word Bird. I have a puzzle for you."

Mama put

n with ap

What word did Mama make?

Word Bird did not
read the word.

He was already
taking a nap.

You can read more word
puzzles with

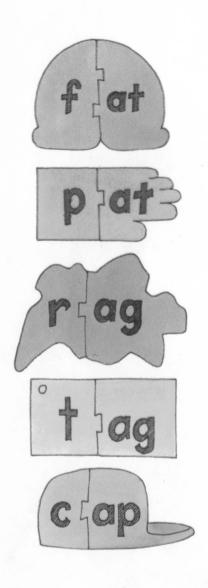

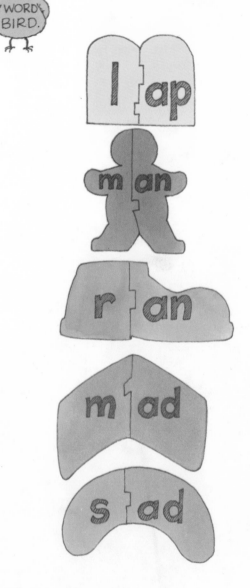

Now you make some
word puzzles.